How the
Narwhal
Got Its Tusk

retold by Alejandro Segovia

illustrated by Dennis Albetski

McGraw-Hill
School Division

New York   Farmington

Narwhals are whales that have a twisted ivory tusk sticking out the front of their heads. Legend has it that the narwhal didn't always have a long tusk. This is the story of how long ago, in a cold and snowy place, narwhals got their tusks.

Once upon a time, in the far north, there were a brother and sister who lived with their aunt. No matter how hard the children tried to please her, she was never happy.

The brother was an excellent hunter. He gave food to his family and to many other families in his village. Every year his neighbors held a feast with the food the boy had caught. But this did not make the aunt happy. Instead it made her angry.

One day the boy brought home the skin of a seal he had caught. The boy's aunt said, "Give me that skin!"

But the boy refused to give her the skin. "I need the skin," he told his aunt. "I must make lines for my harpoon. If I don't, I won't be able to hunt for our food."

The aunt was very angry. But she pretended
to be calm. "I will help you prepare the skin,"
she told the boy. But as she scraped and
cleaned the skin, she whispered to it, "When he
bites you with his knife, you must jump and bite
him back."

When the aunt had finished cleaning the
smooth skin, the boy began to cut the skin for
lines. Suddenly, the seal skin snapped across
the boy's face. When he opened his eyes, he
could no longer see!

When the people in the village heard about
the poor boy, they brought bear meat and whale
meat for him to eat. But the aunt never gave the
boy any meat, and would not let his sister give
him any either. Instead, the boy had to eat
shellfish all winter long.

One spring day, the boy was waiting for his sister to return home. Suddenly he heard someone calling him.

"This way, this way, follow my words," the voice said. So the boy did. Soon the voice was right in front of him. It was loud and clear.

"Hold on to my neck," the voice said. As the boy reached out, he realized that he was holding on to a loon. "Hold your breath and don't swallow any water," the bird said. Then it dove deep into an icy lake. The loon dove right down to the bottom. Then it brought the boy back to the surface.

The bird dove down to the bottom two more times. Then it returned to shore. The boy shook himself off. He knew that something amazing had happened. He could see again!

"Go home," the loon told the boy. "Tomorrow, when you go hunting, you must take your aunt with you."

The boy returned home to his aunt and his
sister. When the aunt found out that the boy
could see again, she was angrier than ever.
When the boy asked her to hunt with him in the
morning, she agreed to go. But she had a plan.

"Tomorrow I will let him catch a whale. Then
I will have enough meat to last a very long time,"
she thought to herself. "When he is done, I will
leave him alone on the vast tundra. Then I will
be rid of him once and for all."

The next morning, the boy and his aunt set out for the ocean. The boy threw his harpoon at the smaller whales. But this wasn't good enough for the aunt.

"You must catch a bigger fish than that!" she yelled. "Try to get an adult whale."

"To do that, I will need your help," the boy cried. "Let me tie my harpoon line around you. Then, when I catch a whale, we can pull it into land." The aunt was so greedy that she agreed to the boy's plan. She helped him to tie the harpoon line around her waist.

The boy
threw his harpoon and hooked a
big whale. But with a flick of its tail, the
big mammal pulled the aunt into the water.
Beneath the surface, the aunt twisted this way
and that. Slowly, she changed into a narwhal.
Her braid became a long, twisted tusk. She
swam far away and was never seen again.

The boy returned to the house and told his
sister that their mean aunt was gone forever.
The boy went back to hunting for food for the
village, and the village in turn took care of the
boy and his sister. The two of them all but
forgot the narwhal that roamed the seas alone.
They lived happily ever after.